THE
MAGNIFICENT
BOOK OF
MONSTERS

THE
MAGNIFICENT
BOOK OF
MONSTERS

ILLUSTRATED BY
Gonzalo Kenny

WRITTEN BY
Diana Ferguson

weldon**owen**

Written by Diana Ferguson
Illustrated by Gonzalo Kenny
Consultant: Professor Asa Simon Mittman

weldon**owen**

Copyright © Weldon Owen Children's Books, 2023

Published by Weldon Owen Children's Books
An imprint of Weldon Owen International, L.P.
A subsidiary of Insight International, L.P.
PO Box 3088
San Rafael, CA 94912
www.insighteditions.com

Weldon Owen Children's Books:
Editor: George Maudsley
Art Director: Stuart Smith
Senior Production Manager: Greg Steffen
Publisher: Sue Grabham

CEO: Raoul Goff

ISBN: 978-1-68188-875-0

Manufactured, printed and assembled in China
First printing, March 2023.. TOP0323
27 26 25 24 23 1 2 3 4 5

MIX
Paper | Supporting
responsible forestry
FSC® C104723

INTRODUCTION

What do you think of when you hear the word monster? Maybe you imagine a huge, hideous figure that roars and growls and comes out at night? Monsters come in many other shapes and sizes, too, from massive to small. Some resemble strange animals and birds, while others look almost like ordinary people. Find out which monsters have been slain and which still live on in the Earth's mountains, skies, rivers, and lakes.

The Magnificent Book of Monsters takes you on a journey to the four corners of the world to encounter monsters of every kind. Spy on the terrifying Asag, with eyes all over his rocky, toadlike body. Take cover from the Stymphalian Birds, with metal feathers that they fire like arrows. Be on guard for the Vodyanoi, who might drag you into his millpond.

Meet snake-haired Medusa, whose gaze could turn you to stone. Encounter evil Ravana with his 20 arms and 10 heads, and the flying heads that have no bodies at all. Discover gigantic monsters such as the great wolf Fenrir, or small ones like the Tokoloshe, which can creep under your bed at night. Meet a crow that feasts on the corpses of warriors, a devil that is followed by flies, and a water monster that swallows ships whole.

Pluck up your courage and set off on a journey to meet some of the most magnificent monsters in the world.

AT A GLANCE

WHERE IN THE WORLD? Japan

APPEARANCE: Hideous ogres with brightly colored skin

LAIR: Underground realm of the dead

BEHAVIOR: Evil and cruel

SPECIAL POWER: Unlimited ability to do evil

CONTENTS

COATLICUE

- A skirt of coiling rattlesnakes dangles from the waist of Coatlicue (*koh-at-lee-kway*). A necklace of severed human hands and hearts with a large skull pendant hangs from her neck.

- The name of this terrifying Aztec goddess means "serpent skirt."

- Coatlicue has no head. Instead, two serpents rise up from her neck to face each other. She has snake's heads instead of hands and talons instead of toes.

- The goddess lost her head and hands when she was attacked by 400 of her sons. They were angry because she was going to have another child. The blood that gushed from her neck and wrists turned into monstrous snakes.

- Coatlicue is the mother of Huitzilopochtli (*weet-zil-oh-poach-lee*), or the Blue Hummingbird. Huitzilopochtli is the Aztec god of the sun and of war. Wielding his fearsome Fire Serpent, this loyal son slew 400 of his brothers for attacking Coatlicue, and turned them into stars.

- The heads, hands, and skull that Coatlicue wears round her neck show that she likes to feed on corpses, or dead bodies. Like the Earth, she swallows up the dead.

- Coatlicue lives on Coatepec, or Snake Mountain, in the middle of Mexico.

AT A GLANCE

WHERE IN THE WORLD? Mexico

APPEARANCE: Snake head and hands, snake skirt

LAIR: Coatepec

BEHAVIOR: Watchful and patient

SPECIAL POWER: Brings life and death

POLYPHEMUS

- Polyphemus is a cyclops, a type of giant with a single eye in the middle of his forehead. He lives in a deep cave on the island of Sicily.

- This cyclops keeps a flock of sheep in his cave. Every day, he drives them out to graze, and every night he brings them back inside again.

- Pails of sheep's milk stand on the floor of the cave for the giant to drink. There are cheeses drying on the rocky ledges. But Polyphemus's favorite food is a snack of human flesh.

- Polyphemus is the son of the sea god Poseidon and a sea nymph called Thoosa.

- The ancient Greek hero Odysseus and 12 of his men once landed on Polyphemus's island. The greedy cyclops found them inside his lair and gobbled up six of them as if they were no more than scraps of chicken.

- Polyphemus has to sniff out his human victims or grope for them in the dark. He cannot see them because he was blinded long ago by the hero Odysseus, who drove a burning stake into the giant's only eye.

AT A GLANCE

WHERE IN THE WORLD? Sicily

APPEARANCE: Single eye in his forehead

LAIR: Cave

BEHAVIOR: Greedy and slow-witted

SPECIAL POWER: Brute strength

TSUCHIGUMO

- Tsuchigumos are huge, monstrous spiders. With eight hairy spider's legs, they have the faces of demons and the bodies of tigers. Their mouths are filled with sharp fangs, perfect for piercing the soft bodies of their prey.

- These monsters hide in dark, secret places in the mountains, caves, and forests of Japan.

- The word tsuchigumo means "earth spider" in Japanese. The creatures make burrows lined with spider's silk in the earth. There they lurk, waiting to ambush their prey.

- Unwary travelers passing through the forest can fall victim to a tsuchigumo. Before they know it, they are seized by this giant beast.

- If they cannot catch a human to eat, tsuchigumos will hunt whatever living creature they can find.

- These demon spiders can take human form to trick their victims.

- Legend has it that a tsuchigumo once transformed itself into a beautiful woman to fool the Japanese hero Yorimitsu. When she changed back into a spider, he slashed her with his famous sword. Thousands of human skulls and baby spiders spilled out of her body.

AT A GLANCE

WHERE IN THE WORLD? Japan

APPEARANCE: Part spider, tiger, and demon

LAIR: Underground tunnel

BEHAVIOR: Cunning and secretive

SPECIAL POWER: Can take human form

BEHEMOTH

- Behemoth is as old as the world itself. He is the ruler of all the animals and birds.

- This gigantic land monster has curved tusks, bones like bronze, and limbs as strong as iron. His bushy tail is bigger than the trunk of a cedar tree.

- This beast lives in the Thousand Mountains, in the lands east of the Mediterranean Sea. When he sleeps, he lies among the reeds, ferns, water lilies, and willows there.

- Every day, Behemoth eats up all the mountain grass until not a blade is left. The next day, all the grass has grown back again. The creature feasts on animals, too.

- In the heat of summer, Behemoth gets so thirsty that he drinks the rivers dry in a single gulp.

AT A GLANCE

WHERE IN THE WORLD?
East of the Mediterranean Sea

APPEARANCE: Massive size and strength

LAIR: Mountains

BEHAVIOR: Commanding but kind

SPECIAL POWER: Controls all wildlife

Once a year in midsummer, Behemoth rears up on his hind legs and lets out a mighty roar that can be heard around the world. It is Behemoth's command to all the wild animals, telling them not to prey on people's sheep and cattle.

No human can conquer Behemoth. But one day the beast will meet his archenemy, the sea monster Leviathan, on the sea shore. The whole world will shudder and shake as the pair rip each other apart.

MAHISHASURA

- Mahishasura was an evil *asura*, or demon, who lived long ago in India. He had the body of a man but the head of a buffalo. The name Mahishasura means "buffalo demon."

- This cunning demon was a clever shape-shifter. He could transform himself into a man, a lion, an elephant, or a giant buffalo.

- For years, Mahishasura worshipped the great god Brahma in the hope that he would be made immortal. Brahma could not make that promise. But he did declare that the demon would never die at the hands of a man.

- With a huge army of fellow demons, Mahishasura terrorized people on Earth, robbing and killing at will. No one was safe.

- Mahishasura and his demons dared to attack the gods. The gods threw their magic discus, club, and thunderbolt at Mahishasura, but nothing could stop him.

- Only a woman could kill Mahishasura. By combining all their energy, the gods created a terrifying 10-handed goddess called Durga. After a fierce battle that raged for nine days, Durga sliced off Mahishasura's head with a magical discus given to her by the gods.

AT A GLANCE

WHERE IN THE WORLD? India

APPEARANCE: Part man, part buffalo

LAIR: In the underworld

BEHAVIOR: Proud and evil

SPECIAL POWERS: Could change shape, almost immortal

FENRIR

- The great wolf Fenrir lives far away in the icy north. Chained to a rock, he tugs and pulls to break free. But he cannot escape because he is bound by a magical chain.

- The magical chain that imprisons Fenrir was crafted by dwarves. They made it from the beard of a woman, the sound of a cat's footsteps, the breath of a fish, the nerves of a bear, and the spit of a bird. The chain is called Gleipnir the Entangler.

- Mighty Fenrir is the son of the god Loki and the giantess Angrboda.

- Fenrir is monstrously huge. His open jaws stretch from the sky above to the earth below. So much saliva drools from his mouth that it has formed a river.

AT A GLANCE

WHERE IN THE WORLD? Scandinavia

APPEARANCE: Huge size, massive drooling jaws

LAIR: Chained to a rock

BEHAVIOR: Angry and unforgiving

SPECIAL POWER: Tremendous strength

It is said that Fenrir will only break free when the world ends. Then the beast will devour Odin, father of all the gods. His wolf sons, Skoll and Hati, will swallow the Sun and Moon, and the whole world will go dark.

STYMPHALIAN BIRDS

- These fearsome birds of prey lived long ago in the marshlands of Lake Stymphalia in ancient Greece. They attacked and devoured any living thing that came their way, including humans.

- The Stymphalian Birds had beaks and claws of bronze, and metal feathers with tips as sharp as nails. They used their feathers as weapons, firing them at their victims like a shower of arrows. The feathers could even pierce armor.

- Crops growing near Lake Stymphalia withered away beneath the birds' poisonous dung. People were afraid to graze their sheep and cattle there for fear of being attacked. The monsters terrorized everyone around them.

- Sometimes hundreds of Stymphalian Birds soared up from the marshes, with their beaks clacking and their feathers clattering. These flocks were so vast that they blotted out the sun.

- The Stymphalian Birds are said to have been created by Ares, the ancient Greek god of war.

AT A GLANCE

WHERE IN THE WORLD? Greece

APPEARANCE: Metal beaks, claws, and feathers

LAIR: Lake Stymphalia

BEHAVIOR: Ravenous and fierce

SPECIAL POWER: Arrowlike wings

The only way to survive an attack of Stymphalian Birds was to wear clothes made of thick cork. The birds' beaks would get stuck in the cork when they tried to peck at their victim's flesh.

The ancient Greek hero Heracles finally slew the terrible birds. He climbed up a mountain to avoid sinking into the swamp where the birds lived, and shook a big rattle to disturb them. As the birds rose into the air, Heracles shot them down with his arrows.

It is said that a few Stymphalian Birds survive to this day on an island in the Black Sea.

ASAG

🐾 The monster Asag lived many thousands of years ago. He was so hideous that his mere presence made fish boil alive in the rivers.

🐾 Asag's toadlike body looked as if it was made from lumps of rock. Nothing could pierce his stony skin. He had three arms, three legs, and no neck. Several glaring eyes were scattered across his body.

🐾 This terrifying rock monster had rock-monster children who looked just like him. They followed him whenever he went into battle.

🐾 Asag was the child of the earth goddess Ki and the sky god An.

🐾 The beast's hideaway was in the caverns and gullies of the mountains, where he lived with his rock-monster children.

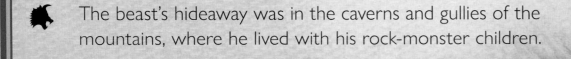

AT A GLANCE

WHERE IN THE WORLD? Sumeria (modern Iraq)

APPEARANCE: Hideous, rocky-skinned, and toadlike

LAIR: Mountains

BEHAVIOR: Loved to cause suffering

SPECIAL POWERS: Caused disease, controlled weather

Asag brought death and disease to the world. He gave people headaches and fevers, and carried death with him. He could also cause droughts and bring freezing weather.

People believed that Asag could never be stopped. But the Sumerian god Ninurta finally slayed him using Sharur, his talking mace. This magical club could fly through the air, talking to Ninurta as it speeded toward its target.

THE NIAN

- Most of the year, the Nian lives in the depths of the ocean. But on the last day of the year, he rises up through the stormy waves. He comes ashore in search of tasty humans to eat.

- This Chinese monster is called the Nian because he appears just once a year. *Nian* is the Chinese word for year.

- The Nian is like no other monster you have ever seen. He has the face and body of a lion, and spears his prey with the huge horn on his head. His razor-sharp fangs are perfect for tearing and ripping flesh.

- When the Nian opens his jaws wide, he can gulp down more than one person at a time. If he cannot find people to devour, he will eat livestock instead.

AT A GLANCE

WHERE IN THE WORLD? China

APPEARANCE: Lionlike with a horn and fangs

LAIR: Bottom of the ocean

BEHAVIOR: Greedy but can be fearful

SPECIAL POWER: Survives for months underwater

There are only three things that the Nian fears—bright lights, fireworks, and the color red. To keep the creature at bay, decorate your home with red lanterns and scrolls, and let off fireworks at New Year.

At New Year, it is traditional to make a model of the Nian out of bamboo, paper, and cloth. The model is paraded through the streets and drums, cymbals, and gongs are used to scare the real Nian away.

MISHIPESHU

- Mishipeshu lives in the darkest depths of Lake Superior, the largest freshwater lake in the world.

- This monster's name means "Great Lynx." Mishipeshu has the head and paws of a giant cat and the horns of a bison. Spines run along the back and tail of his scaly body.

- Mishipeshu whips up storms as he slithers through the water. He churns up the lake until it looks like a boiling cauldron. Any boats out on the water are swallowed up by the waves.

- In winter, Mishipeshu sometimes breaks the ice that forms on the lake. This is to make those walking on the ice fall into the freezing water underneath and drown.

- Sometimes you can hear the Great Lynx's angry hiss. It sounds like rushing water.

- Mishipeshu guards a hoard of precious copper on Michipicoten (*mi-ship-i-cote-un*) Island. This magical island is surrounded by drifting fog, which makes the land appear to float above the water.

- Some have tried to steal Mishipeshu's copper hoard. But the water monster has pursued them and sunk their ship before they could reach land.

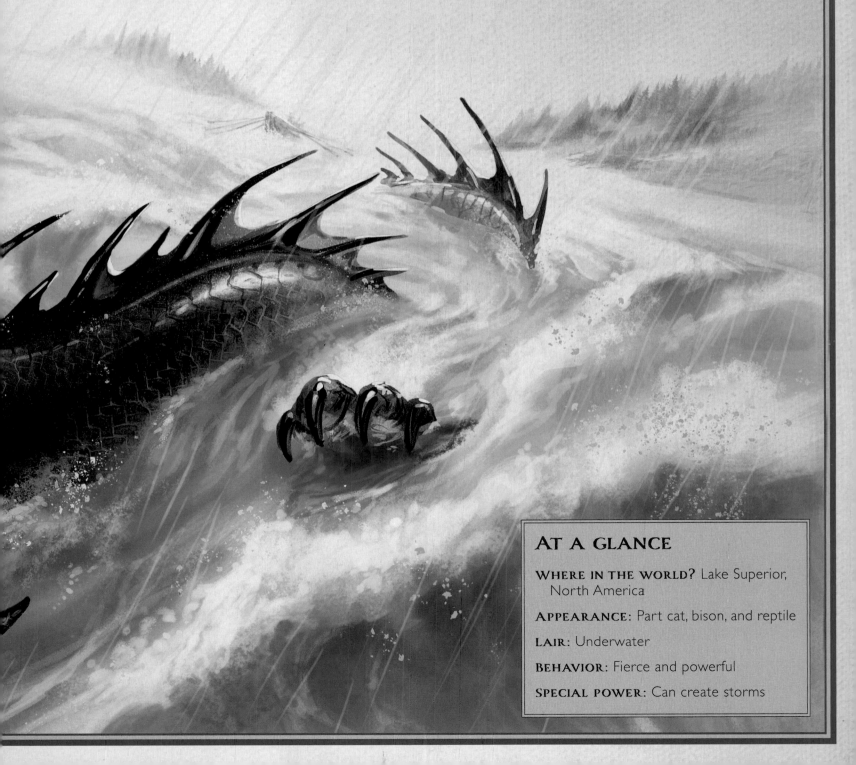

AT A GLANCE

WHERE IN THE WORLD? Lake Superior, North America

APPEARANCE: Part cat, bison, and reptile

LAIR: Underwater

BEHAVIOR: Fierce and powerful

SPECIAL POWER: Can create storms

THE MINOTAUR

- With the body of a man and the head and tail of a bull, the Minotaur was a hideous sight. But unlike a bull, this monster did not graze on grass. Instead, he gorged himself on human flesh.

- The Minotaur lived long ago in a dark and winding labyrinth beneath the royal palace on the island of Crete. Minos, king of Crete, had built the underground labyrinth to hide the monster away, deep in the heart of the maze.

- Every year, seven boys and seven girls were sent from the city of Athens as a sacrifice to the Minotaur. Trapped inside the twists and turns of the monster's lair, they waited to be devoured, one by one.

- Theseus, son of the king of Athens, went to Crete to kill the Minotaur. He met the gruesome monster in the middle of his maze. A terrifying struggle followed, but in the end the Minotaur lay dead at the hero's feet.

- Ariadne, daughter of King Minos, wanted to help the Greek hero Theseus slay the Minotaur. She gave Theseus a ball of thread, which he unwound as he went into the Minotaur's maze. After killing the beast, he followed the thread back out. Without it, he would have been lost forever.

AT A GLANCE

WHERE IN THE WORLD? Crete

APPEARANCE: Part bull, part man

LAIR: Underground labyrinth

BEHAVIOR: Savage and starving

SPECIAL POWER: Stupendous strength

THE MORRÍGAN

- The Morrígan is the Irish goddess of war and death. She flies over battlefields in the form of a huge black crow. Warriors who see her are terrified, for it means they will soon die.

- Disguised as a crow, the Morrígan descends to the battlefield to feast on the corpses that lie there. She pecks out their eyes and pulls the flesh off their bones until they are bare.

- This powerful goddess is a cunning shape-shifter. As well as taking the form of a crow, she can turn herself into an eel, an enormous wolf, a cow, a beautiful young woman, or an old crone.

- The Morrígan does not always bring death. Sometimes she comes to the aid of warriors instead. She spurs them to fight harder for victory so that they do not die.

AT A GLANCE

WHERE IN THE WORLD? Ireland

APPEARANCE: Crow and other forms

LAIR: Mounds and hills of Ireland

BEHAVIOR: Loves war and death

SPECIAL POWERS: Shape-shifting and foretelling death

Some people have seen the Morrígan disguised as an old washerwoman crone, washing the bloodstained clothes of those who will die in battle.

The Morrígan can appear as just one woman, or she can split herself into three. The names of these three sisters are Badb (*baib*), Macha (*maj-er*) and Nemain (*nay-van*).

The Morrígan's husband is the Dagda, warrior-king of the Irish gods. He owns three magical treasures—a cauldron that never runs out of food, a club that can bring the dead back to life, and a harp that can make people laugh, cry, or sleep.

BUNYIP

- Many are too afraid to describe a bunyip. Those who aren't scared say it looks like a hairy seal or a hippopotamus with a bulldog's head. Others believe that it looks more like an alligator or large bird. Everyone is sure of one thing—that a bunyip is big enough to eat a human being.

- Bunyips live in the swamps, streams, lagoons, and billabongs, or pools, of Australia.

- At night, bunyips come out of the water to hunt. They prowl the dry land looking for prey. Women and children are their favorite food. Sometimes bunyips kill their victims by hugging them to death.

AT A GLANCE

WHERE IN THE WORLD? Australia

APPEARANCE: Seallike or hippolike body and doglike head

LAIR: Swamps, streams, billabongs

BEHAVIOR: Fearless and greedy

SPECIAL POWERS: Controls water levels, has paralyzing roar

A bunyip's roar echoes through the air at night. Its sound can paralyze anyone who gets too close.

Bunyips have magical powers. They can change the water levels in the swamps and pools where they live.

A bunyip lays enormous pale blue eggs. It hides them in platypus nests, tucked into the banks of streams and rivers.

THE CUEGLE

- The Cuegle roams the hills and mountains of Cantabria in northern Spain, striking fear into the hearts of the people who live there.

- Part human, part monster, the creature shuffles along on two short legs. It has three arms but no hands or fingers. With its dark face, gray hair, long beard, and single horn, it is a terrifying sight.

- The Cuegle peers out at the world with its three eyes. One eye is yellow, one red, and one blue. Five rows of teeth fill the monster's jaws, ready to rip into flesh.

- Few living creatures are safe from the Cuegle. It attacks livestock and people. Worst of all, it loves to steal babies from their cradles.

- Although it is small, the Cuegle is incredibly strong. It can easily overcome any human who confronts it. The best way to keep safe is to stay out of the Cuegle's way.

- The only weapons that can fend off the Cuegle are oak and holly leaves. The monster hates these plants and will not come near them. Mothers place oak and holly leaves in their babies' cradles to keep their infants safe.

AT A GLANCE

WHERE IN THE WORLD? Cantabria, Spain

APPEARANCE: Part human, part animal

LAIR: Mountains

BEHAVIOR: Stealthy and sneaky

SPECIAL POWER: Overwhelming strength

BASKET OGRESS

- When the Basket Ogress sighs, it sounds like the wind rushing through the forest. She is on the prowl for her next meal.

- The Basket Ogress is a terrifying giant who likes to eat children. Some people know her by the name Dzunukwa (*zoo-noo-kwah*).

- This hideous creature is very old, with a bent back. She stoops over as she walks. Her skin is wrinkled and her hair is long, bushy, and tangled.

- The Ogress snatches children and puts them into the large basket she carries on her back. She can fit in as many as six children at a time.

- The Basket Ogress's lips are always set in an O-shape. Her cry sounds like "Hu, hu!"

- This flesh-eating giant brings her victims back to her hut deep in the woods. Here, she will roast them slowly over the fire.

- Although she is big and strong, the Ogress is not very smart. If children are clever and act quickly, most will escape her clutches.

AT A GLANCE

WHERE IN THE WORLD? Northwest coast of North America

APPEARANCE: Old, wrinkled giant

LAIR: Hut in the forest

BEHAVIOR: Tireless and hungry

SPECIAL POWER: Ability to catch many children

THE MINOKAWA

- This monstrous bird lives far away, beyond the place where the Sun rises. The Minokawa never sleeps. He is always waiting for the chance to do evil deeds.

- The Minokawa is almost as big as the sky itself. His feathers are as sharp as swords and his beak and legs are as strong as steel. His eyes glitter like two shining mirrors.

- The Minokawa lies in wait for the Moon to rise. He wants to snatch it in his gigantic beak and swallow it whole. Once he has devoured the Moon, he will try to gulp down the Sun.

- Sometimes the Minokawa nibbles only part of the Moon. This turns the Moon a reddish-brown color, which can last for hours.

- Even the Moon and Sun are not enough to fill this ravenous monster's belly. He is so hungry that he might try to eat all the people on Earth, too.

AT A GLANCE

WHERE IN THE WORLD? Philippines

APPEARANCE: Gigantic bird with metal beak and legs, and mirror eyes

LAIR: Beyond the eastern horizon

BEHAVIOR: Hungry and patient

SPECIAL POWER: Can swallow the Moon

There is one way to stop this monster. When he starts to eat the Moon, people must yell and scream and bang drums loudly. The noise will startle the Minokawa, who will open his beak, giving the Moon a chance to escape.

TOKOLOSHE

- Some monsters are huge, but a tokoloshe is small enough to creep under your bed. But do not be fooled by the size of this demon—it is highly dangerous.

- A tokoloshe looks like a goblin, with a big head, large eyes, and a skinny, hairy body. It can make itself invisible by drinking water or by swallowing a stone.

- Tokoloshes live in streams and pools but come out at night. They sneak into bedrooms and suck the life out of people while they sleep. If a person is lucky, a tokoloshe will only bite off their toes.

- A tokoloshe can be summoned by a witch to do someone harm. If horrible things suddenly happen to someone you know, a tokoloshe may well be to blame.

- Tokoloshes like stealing milk from cows, and have been seen escaping from cow sheds.

- Witches can tame these creatures by cutting the fringe that hangs over their eyes and by feeding them milk, which tokoloshes love.

- One way to protect yourself from a tokoloshe is to raise your bed on bricks. This prevents the demon from reaching you while you sleep.

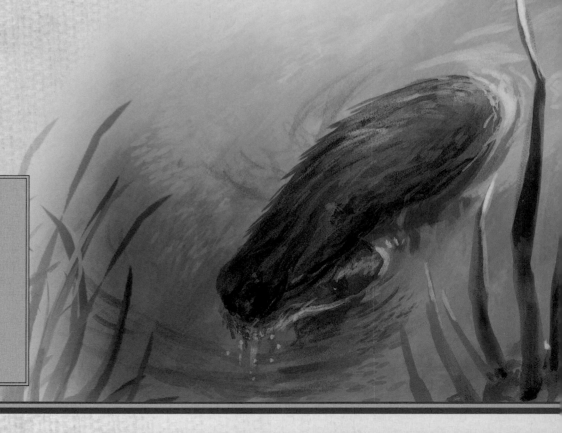

AT A GLANCE

WHERE IN THE WORLD?
Southern Africa

APPEARANCE: Goblinlike

LAIR: Water

BEHAVIOR: Mischievous and evil

SPECIAL POWER: Sucks life from its victims

MANTICORE

- The fierce, flesh-eating manticore lives in Iran and the rainforests of India. All the people there fear it, for manticore means man-eater.

- The manticore has the head of a bearded man but the body and claws of a lion. Its jaws are lined with three rows of razor-sharp teeth. But its most terrifying weapon is its scorpionlike tail, edged with venomous spines.

- This cunning predator hides in the reeds and grasses with only its human face showing. It waits for an unwary person to come close by, then leaps out and crushes them in its monstrous jaws.

AT A GLANCE

WHERE IN THE WORLD? India and Iran

APPEARANCE: Human face, lion's body, and scorpion's tail

LAIR: Rainforest

BEHAVIOR: Ferocious, cunning, ravenous

SPECIAL POWER: Arrowlike tail spines

A manticore sometimes hunts its victims, shooting at them with the spines on its tail like arrows from a bow. The poisonous spines paralyze the victim so they cannot escape. For every spine that the manticore shoots, a new one grows.

A single human is no more than a light snack for a manticore. This hungry monster prefers to eat three or more people at once. It devours every last scrap—flesh, teeth, eyes, hair, bones—until nothing is left.

The only creature a manticore cannot conquer is the elephant.

This powerful beast can run at lightning speed. Its call sounds like a trumpet. It booms through the forest, terrifying anyone who hears it.

SCYLLA

- Sailors dread traveling through the Strait of Messina, a narrow sea channel between Sicily and Italy. This is where Scylla lurks, waiting to pluck her victims from their ships and eat them alive.

- Six heads on long, snaky necks rise from Scylla's shoulders. Each head is armed with three rows of shark teeth. Howling dogs' heads surround the monster's waist.

- Once, Scylla was a beautiful sea nymph, but the sorceress Circe threw magic herbs into the water where Scylla was bathing. She instantly turned into a hideous monster.

- Scylla hides in a deep cavern on the side of a cliff, waiting and watching. As soon as anyone comes within reach, her long necks shoot out to snatch up her victims.

- Terrifying Scylla once snatched six sailors from the crew of the ancient Greek hero Odysseus. As their ship passed by her cave, she stretched out her necks, grabbed one sailor in each mouth, and devoured the screaming men whole.

AT A GLANCE

WHERE IN THE WORLD? Strait of Messina, Sicily

APPEARANCE: Six heads and 12 legs

LAIR: Cliffside cavern

BEHAVIOR: Watchful and greedy

SPECIAL POWER: Lightning-fast attack

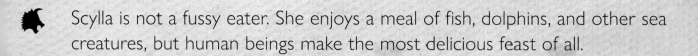 Scylla is not a fussy eater. She enjoys a meal of fish, dolphins, and other sea creatures, but human beings make the most delicious feast of all.

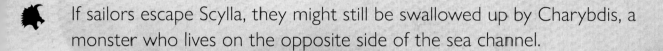 If sailors escape Scylla, they might still be swallowed up by Charybdis, a monster who lives on the opposite side of the sea channel.

FLYING HEAD

- Flying heads come out at night, when the thunder roars, the lightning flashes, and the wind howls. They roam through the sky, looking for humans to eat.

- These terrifying monsters have no bodies. Their long, matted hair streams out behind them like the wings of some great bird of prey.

- The flying head can sniff out the tiniest whiff of human flesh. With its jaws clacking and its mouth drooling, the monster is always ready to feast.

- Flying heads live in northeastern North America. An attack by these monsters has been known to wipe out whole villages.

- Some people say that these monsters are the severed heads of killed people. Some say they are human cannibals transformed into hideous heads. But others say that these creatures are just the spirits of the wind.

AT A GLANCE

WHERE IN THE WORLD? Northeast North America

APPEARANCE: Head with no body

LAIR: Storms

BEHAVIOR: Ravenous and slow-witted

SPECIAL POWER: Ability to fly

There is one way to trick a flying head. Heat some stones on a fire and pretend to eat them. The greedy creature will gobble up the stones, which will burn its mouth. Screaming in pain, it will fly away, never to be seen again.

AMMIT

- Monstrous Ammit is feared by all who are about to die. She is known as the Devourer of the Dead, the Bone Eater, and the Eater of Hearts. Her favorite food is a human heart.

- Ammit has the head of a crocodile. The front part of her body looks like a lion's. The rear looks like a hippo's.

- This fearsome creature lives in the Egyptian underworld, where the dead come after they die.

- Ammit sits beneath the Scales of Justice. She waits for the dead to have their hearts weighed in the hope that she will get one to eat. The heart of a good person is as light as a feather. The heart of a bad person is heavy. Only the hearts of bad people are eaten by Ammit.

AT A GLANCE

WHERE IN THE WORLD? Egypt

APPEARANCE: Part crocodile, part lion, part hippo

LAIR: Egyptian underworld

BEHAVIOR: Eager for human hearts

SPECIAL POWER: Turns people into ghosts

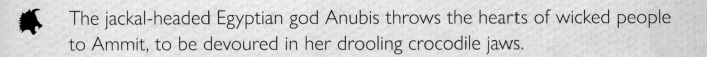

The jackal-headed Egyptian god Anubis throws the hearts of wicked people to Ammit, to be devoured in her drooling crocodile jaws.

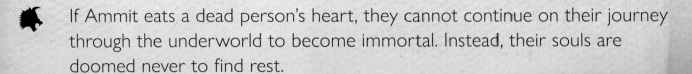

If Ammit eats a dead person's heart, they cannot continue on their journey through the underworld to become immortal. Instead, their souls are doomed never to find rest.

RAVANA

- Evil Ravana lived long ago. He was king of a horde of foul demons called the Rakshashas. Ravana had the power to make himself invisible and was a master of disguise, able to take on any shape he wished.

- Ravana had 20 arms and 10 heads. He could wield a different weapon in each of his 20 hands. If anyone cut off one of his heads, a new one would instantly sprout in its place.

- A fortress on the island of Sri Lanka was the demon king's home. From here, he took to the air in a flying chariot to travel through the sky.

- If Ravana got angry, he could cause storms and earthquakes.

- One day, Ravana became enraged with the god Shiva and shook the mountain on which he was sitting. Shiva gently placed his toe on the ground and the whole mountain tumbled down on top of Ravana, trapping him underneath it for 1,000 years.

- Ravana kidnapped Sita, wife of the god Rama. After days of battle to win her back, Rama finally killed the demon king with the fiery tip of a magic arrow.

AT A GLANCE

WHERE IN THE WORLD? Sri Lanka

APPEARANCE: Twenty arms and 10 heads

LAIR: Fortress on Sri Lanka

BEHAVIOR: Evil and angry

SPECIAL POWERS: Could become invisible, take any shape, and caused storms and earthquakes

MEDUSA

This hideous monster lived thousands of years ago on a remote island in the far west of the ancient Greek world, in the place where the sun sets.

Medusa was a Gorgon, a type of winged female monster. She had a lolling tongue, fearsome pig's tusks, and writhing snakes instead of hair. But her staring eyes were the most terrifying of all, for they could turn someone to stone with a single glance.

Medusa had two Gorgon sisters called Stheno and Euryale. Her sisters were immortal and would never die. Only Medusa could be slain.

The ancient Greek hero Perseus set out to kill Medusa. To help him, he had a helmet that made him invisible, winged sandals that allowed him to fly, and a shield as shiny as glass.

To kill Medusa, Perseus used a shiny shield given to him by the goddess Athena. Instead of looking into Medusa's eyes, which would turn him to stone, he looked at her reflection in the shield. Using the reflection to guide him, he sliced off her head with his curved sword.

A fountain of blood spurted from Medusa's neck when the hero Perseus cut off her head. Out of the foaming blood sprang the winged horse Pegasus and the giant Chryasor.

AT A GLANCE

WHERE IN THE WORLD? Greece

APPEARANCE: Hideous face with pig's tusks and snake hair

LAIR: Island in the far west

BEHAVIOR: Fiercely defensive

SPECIAL POWER: Eyes that could turn you to stone

ROC

- The Roc is so huge that it can seize an elephant in its enormous talons. It carries off the animal into the wide blue sky to devour later. The Roc also likes to feast on giant snakes.

- The wingspan of this gigantic bird is seven times wider than the largest eagle's. Its wing feathers are as big as palm leaves and its legs are as thick as tree trunks.

- Moving at lightning speed, the Roc sometimes flies in front of the Sun, blocking its light and turning day to night.

- The Roc never lands anywhere except on Mount Qaf. This remote and mysterious mountain shimmers with a greenish-blue glow, and is said to be made of emeralds. It is where magical genies live.

- The Roc's egg is smooth and white, and bigger than 250 hen's eggs. Some have mistaken it for the Sun.

AT A GLANCE

WHERE IN THE WORLD?
Southwest Asia

APPEARANCE: Gigantic bird

LAIR: Mountaintop nest

BEHAVIOR: Hardly ever lands

SPECIAL POWER: Huge size and strength

The famous Arabian sailor Sinbad once came across the Roc by accident. To escape, he secretly tied himself to the bird's leg with his turban. When the Roc flew low over the land, Sinbad untied himself and got away.

VODYANOI

- If you go near water at night, be on the lookout for a vodyanoi. This evil creature may be waiting to grab you and drag you down into its watery lair.

- A cunning vodyanoi can take many forms. It might look like an old man with a green beard, burning eyes, webbed paws, and a fish's tail. A vodyanoi can also disguise itself as a hideous fish, a man covered with moss, or a woman combing her wet hair.

- Vodyanois live in lakes, pools, streams, and rivers. But their favorite lair is a millpond—a pool next to a mill. The name vodyanoi comes from *voda*, which is the Russian word for water.

- A vodyanoi grows younger when the Moon is waxing, or getting bigger. It grows older when the Moon is waning, or getting smaller. Its green beard can even turn white.

- Some vodyanois live in mounds of slimy logs underwater. Others dwell in glittering crystal palaces, decorated with gold and silver stolen from shipwrecks. Magic stones as bright as the Sun light the space inside.

- If a vodyanoi catches someone, they will become its servant. But some vodyanois have been known to eat their victims instead.

- To keep themselves safe, fishermen and millers offer gifts to please the vodyanois. Fishermen throw tobacco or butter into the water, while millers give them bread or salt.

AT A GLANCE

WHERE IN THE WORLD? Russia and eastern Europe

APPEARANCE: Various

LAIR: Underwater

BEHAVIOR: Evil and cunning

SPECIAL POWER: Master of disguise

AMAROK

- Padding silently across the snow on his giant paws, the Amarok roams the frozen lands of the Arctic, where the Inuit live.

- Thick, shaggy gray fur covers the wolf's enormous body. His razor-sharp teeth can tear off chunks of flesh, and his bite is so powerful that he can crunch through bone.

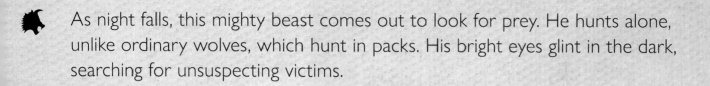 As night falls, this mighty beast comes out to look for prey. He hunts alone, unlike ordinary wolves, which hunt in packs. His bright eyes glint in the dark, searching for unsuspecting victims.

The Amarok stalks any humans who are foolish enough to be out alone at night. With his super senses, he can sniff out a human from a long way away. He leaps upon them before they even know he is there.

In Inuit legend, a lonely boy prayed to the gods for strength. People laughed at him because he was weak. The Amarok came to the boy's aid, wrestling with him every day to make him stronger. Eventually, the boy was strong enough to overpower three bears.

AT A GLANCE

WHERE IN THE WORLD? Arctic regions

APPEARANCE: Huge wolf

LAIR: Cave or underground den

BEHAVIOR: Ferocious but can be kind

SPECIAL POWERS: Super strength and super senses

THE SPHINX

- The ancient Greek Sphinx had the head and chest of a woman, the body of a lion, the wings of an eagle, and the tail of a snake.

- The gods sent the Sphinx to Greece. She originally lived in Ethiopia, in northeast Africa.

- The Sphinx's father was said to be Typhon, a grisly snake-headed giant. Her mother was the dragon Echidna, half-woman and half-snake.

- This fearsome creature sat on Mount Phicium, looking out for travelers on their way to the city of Thebes. People were terrified to pass near her.

AT A GLANCE

WHERE IN THE WORLD? Greece

APPEARANCE: Part human, part animal

LAIR: Mountain cave

BEHAVIOR: Cruel and destructive

SPECIAL POWER: Created nearly impossible riddles

Every traveler who passed the Sphinx's lair had to answer a riddle. If they got the answer wrong, the monster devoured them.

The Sphinx asked passing travelers a riddle—what walks on four legs in the morning, two at noon, and three in the evening? The answer was a person, who crawls on four legs as a baby, walks on two legs as an adult, and uses a stick to walk when they are old.

The Greek hero Oedipus defeated the Sphinx by answering her impossible riddle. In a rage, she threw herself from Mount Phicium and died.

YACUMAMA

- Yacumama lives deep in the heart of the Amazon rainforest. She sometimes lies stretched out on the banks of the great river Amazon, and at other times glides invisibly under the water.

- This giant water serpent is larger than any ordinary river snake. Her head is as big as a person and her body is as long as a blue whale's—or as long as 10 alligators placed head to tail.

- The great serpent's name means "Mother of the Waters" in the Quechua language of Peru. She is the mother of all creatures that live in the water.

- Yacumama controls the temperature of the river water and can create whirlpools and whip up storms.

AT A GLANCE

WHERE IN THE WORLD? Peru

APPEARANCE: Enormous serpent

LAIR: Rivers

BEHAVIOR: Proud and demanding

SPECIAL POWER: Controls rivers and weather

If you go within 100 steps of Yacumama, she will swallow you whole. Locals blow on a conch-shell horn to attract her attention. If she shows herself, they know it is dangerous to go any closer.

The great water mother is said to have created the Boiling River, a tributary of the river Amazon. This steaming river is scalding hot and the muddy banks can burn your feet.

Yacumama can be soothed with gifts of food or drink.

BEELZEBUB

- Beelzebub is one of the most powerful of all devils. He was once worshipped as a god by the people of the ancient city of Ekron, in what is now Israel. Although the city is gone, Beelzebub remains as mighty as ever.

- Wherever he goes, Beelzebub is followed by hordes of buzzing flies. He is sometimes known as the Lord of the Flies. He is also known as God of Filth and the Lord of Dung.

- The flies that trail Beelzebub feed on filth and swarm around the rotting bodies of the dead. The flies lay their eggs in the decaying flesh, hatch, and rise up to spread disease.

- With his horns and wings, Beelzebub looks like a typical devil. But he can also take the form of an enormous fly.

- The Lord of the Flies causes trouble and brings destruction wherever he goes. He can take control of people and make them do wicked things. The more suffering Beelzebub causes, the happier he is.

- Beelzebub lives in Hell, the underworld of the dead. Hell is ruled by Satan, the Devil himself. Beelzebub and Satan could be one and the same.

AT A GLANCE

WHERE IN THE WORLD? Palestine (modern Israel)

APPEARANCE: Devil's horns and wings, or flylike

LAIR: Hell

BEHAVIOR: Loves to cause suffering

SPECIAL POWER: Can take possession of people

CHARYBDIS

- This ancient Greek sea monster lives beneath a cliff by the sea. Charybdis is always thirsty. Three times a day she drinks the sea dry. Three times a day she spits it back out again. The water comes roaring and swirling back up like a boiling cauldron.

- Charybdis can swallow ships whole, along with everyone on board. Nothing remains except a few scraps floating on the surface.

- The all-powerful ancient Greek sea god Poseidon is Charybdis's father. Her mother is the great Earth goddess, Gaia.

AT A GLANCE

WHERE IN THE WORLD? Strait of Messina, Sicily

APPEARANCE: Enormous whirlpool

LAIR: Beneath a cliff

BEHAVIOR: Always thirsty

SPECIAL POWER: Can swallow ships whole

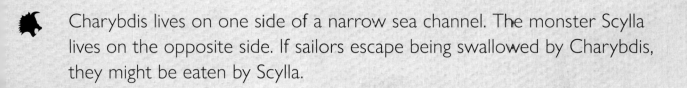 Charybdis lives on one side of a narrow sea channel. The monster Scylla lives on the opposite side. If sailors escape being swallowed by Charybdis, they might be eaten by Scylla.

The Greek hero Odysseus was almost sucked into the monster's gaping mouth when she swallowed the sea, along with his raft. He clung to a fig tree on a cliff and waited until Charybdis spewed the raft back out.

HUMBABA

- This hideous monster lived thousands of years ago in Mesopotamia.

- Snakelike coils covered Humbaba's face and thorny scales cloaked his body. Instead of hands and feet, he had lion's paws and vulture's claws. Bull horns sprouted from his head, and his tail ended in a snake's head.

- Humbaba was the guardian of the Cedar Forest in ancient Mesopotamia. The air here was filled with the scent of the cedar trees, and the gods lived on a mountain in the middle. Human beings were forbidden from entering the forest.

- The beast's roar was as loud as a rushing flood and his breath was as hot as fire. He could hear the tiniest rustling sound in his forest home even when he was hundreds of miles away.

- Seven magical cloaks gave Humbaba extra power. They radiated a kind of invisible energy that filled his enemies with fear and froze them to the spot.

- The hero Gilgamesh killed Humbaba with the help of the sun god, Shamash. The god sent 13 wind storms against the monster. Humbaba could not withstand this attack, and Gilgamesh was able to cut off his head.

AT A GLANCE

WHERE IN THE WORLD?
Mesopotamia (modern Iraq)

APPEARANCE: Hideous, with animal body parts

LAIR: The Cedar Forest

BEHAVIOR: Fierce and warlike

SPECIAL POWER: Can freeze enemies with fear

THE ROPEN

- The Ropen looks like a prehistoric monster. It has been terrifying the people of Papua New Guinea for hundreds of years. The name Ropen means "demon flyer."

- A horny crest crowns the Ropen's head and its long beak is filled with sharp teeth. Thin skin stretches across the monster's enormous, batlike wings and its stiff, spiny tail ends in a diamond-shaped flap.

- At night, this monster takes to the air on gigantic wings. The Ropen flies from its forested mountain home to coral reefs, where it uses its razor-sharp talons to gorge on fish, squid, and giant clams.

- The Ropen loves to eat human flesh, but not the flesh of the living. It prefers to feast on the dead. This creature might even swoop down on funerals and has been known to dig up newly buried bodies.

- You can see when the Ropen is approaching because it glows in the dark. Sometimes it shimmers so brightly that entire villages are lit up as it passes overhead.

- To protect the dead from the Ropen's desire for dead flesh, it is a good idea to cover up graves with rocks.

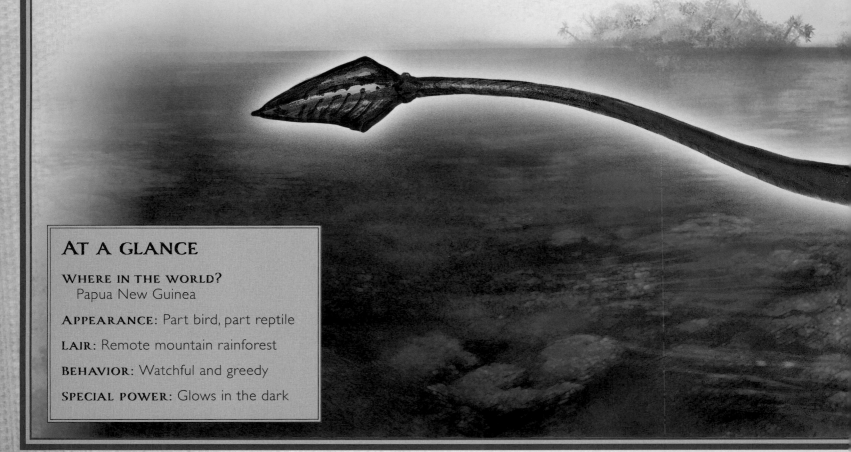

AT A GLANCE

WHERE IN THE WORLD?
Papua New Guinea

APPEARANCE: Part bird, part reptile

LAIR: Remote mountain rainforest

BEHAVIOR: Watchful and greedy

SPECIAL POWER: Glows in the dark

TZITZIMIME

- The Tzitzimime (*zits-im-im-me*) are terrifying Aztec demons that live in the sky. Most of the time, these female monsters look like stars.

- These star demons can take human form. They change into skeletons with skull heads, lolling tongues, and hideous snake's tails. Their skirts are fringed with shells, and their bones clatter as they move about.

- At dawn and dusk, the Tzitzimime attack the Sun to drive it from the sky.

- Occasionally, the Tzitzimime try to devour the Sun during the day. As they clutch and bite, the Sun disappears, causing a solar eclipse. The sky goes dark and day turns into night.

- Solar eclipses are very dangerous times. This is when the Tzitzimime may descend to Earth, diving headlong from the sky like a shower of spiders on silk threads. They want to destroy the world and everyone on it.

- The queen of the star demons is the goddess Itzpapalotl (*itz-pa-pa-lot*).

AT A GLANCE

WHERE IN THE WORLD? Mexico

APPEARANCE: Hideous skeletons

LAIR: The sky

BEHAVIOR: Fierce and destructive

SPECIAL POWER: Can eat the Sun

KELPIE

- A kelpie looks like a beautiful black horse. But before you get too close, take a careful look at its hooves. If they are facing the wrong way, this is not a horse but a kelpie.

- Kelpies live in the streams and rivers of Scotland. Some can be found in Scottish lochs, or lakes.

- These water monsters can take human form, so beware of any person you meet near a stream or river. If they have water weeds in their hair, they might be a kelpie in disguise.

- The kelpie lets you ride on its back. But before you can get off, it will try to gallop off into the water. It is 10 times stronger than a real horse. Using its great strength, it will hold you under the water to devour you, then throw any leftovers onto the bank.

- A kelpie's neck can stretch out to carry as many as nine children at a time. The creature's sticky skin means the children can never climb off.

AT A GLANCE

WHERE IN THE WORLD? Scotland

APPEARANCE: Horselike

LAIR: Streams, rivers, lakes

BEHAVIOR: Cunning and deceitful

SPECIAL POWER: Can take human form

Not all kelpies look the same. Some have manes made of snakes. A kelpie that lives in the River Spey appears as a white horse. It tempts victims onto its back with its strange and beautiful singing.

Kelpies sometimes wear saddles and bridles. If you can pull off a kelpie's bridle, it will become your servant.

The only thing that can kill a kelpie is a silver bullet.

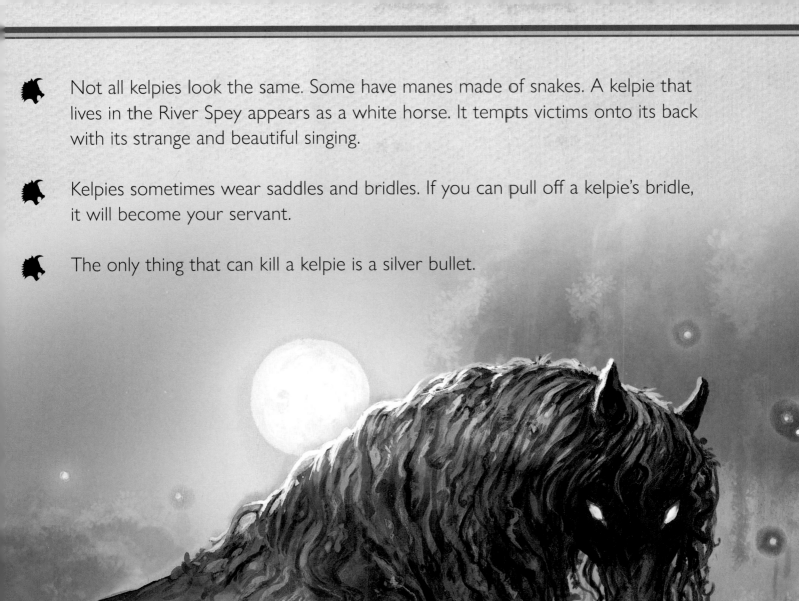

IMPUNDULU

- When dark clouds loom in the sky, it might just be a coming storm. Or it could mean that the terrible Impundulu, the lightning bird, is on its way.

- The flapping of the Impundulu's huge wings sounds like a rumble of thunder. Its claws crackle and flash as they shoot bolts of lightning across the sky.

- The Impundulu is a vampire bird that loves nothing more than drinking people's blood. Its thirst for human blood can never be satisfied. If it cannot get blood, it steals milk instead.

- Most of the time, the Impundulu remains invisible. But it sometimes appears to women as a huge bird. Its feathers may be black or white, or red and white. Sometimes, the Impundulu appears as a handsome man.

- The Impundulu is sometimes a witch's servant, employed to do her evil bidding. It might kidnap children or spread the deadly disease tuberculosis.

AT A GLANCE

WHERE IN THE WORLD? South Africa

APPEARANCE: Birdlike

LAIR: The sky

BEHAVIOR: Bloodthirsty

SPECIAL POWER: Causes storms

To lay an egg, the Impundulu shoots a bolt of lightning down from the sky. The egg is buried where the lightning hits the ground.

Some have tried to stop the Impundulu by throwing spears at the bird, but no one has succeeded. The only thing that can kill the Impundulu is fire.

ONI

- Oni are the most horrible monsters you could ever meet. There is no end to their wickedness and cruelty.

- These huge, hideous ogres often have blue, red, or green skin, and horns growing out of their heads. Their long fangs and sharp claws are perfect for tearing flesh.

- The only clothes oni wear are loincloths made of tiger skin.

- Oni carry heavy, spiked clubs that they use to attack people. The oni might crush a person's bones or even cook their victims in a frying pan.

- When wicked human beings die, they might be transformed into oni. If a person is especially evil, they may become an oni while they are still alive.

- Oni live in an underground realm called Jigoku. It is ruled by Emma-o, the Japanese lord of death.

- It is possible to kill an oni if you are brave and quick-witted, like the Japanese hero Yorimitsu. He slew the famous oni Shuten-doji, but even after he had cut the monster's head off, it still tried to bite him. Yorimitsu protected himself by stacking several helmets on his head.

- To avoid an oni attack, throw roasted soya beans around your home. A magic mixture of holly leaves and dried sardine heads will also keep these monsters away.

AT A GLANCE

WHERE IN THE WORLD? Japan

APPEARANCE: Hideous ogres with brightly colored skin

LAIR: Underground realm of the dead

BEHAVIOR: Evil and cruel

SPECIAL POWER: Unlimited ability to do evil